Cinderella's ... ɔe

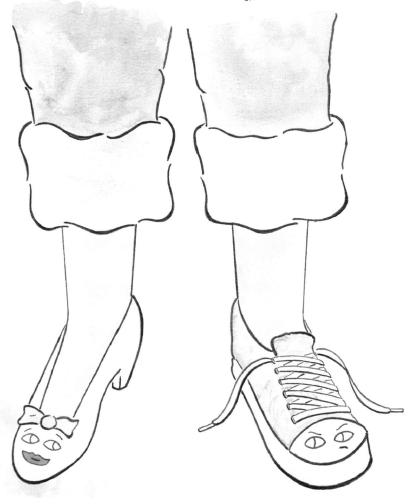

Philippa Rae

Illustrations by Tevin Hansen

Handersen Publishing LLC
Lincoln, Nebraska

Cinderella's Other Shoe

Handersen Publishing, LLC
Lincoln, Nebraska

Text copyright © 2017 Philippa Rae
Illustrations copyright © 2017 Tevin Hansen
Cover copyright © 2017 Handersen Publishing, LLC
Cover Design by Nichole Hansen
Interior Design by Tevin Hansen

Summary: The story of Cinderella told from a shoe's perspective.

Library of Congress Control Number: 2017952671
Handersen Publishing, LLC, Lincoln, Nebraska

ISBN-13: 9781941429884

Publisher Website:
www.handersenpublishing.com
Publisher Email:
editors@handersenpublishing.com

For my very own Prince Charming, Richard.

—Philippa

For my Beautiful Princess and my Handsome Prince, E & G.

—Tevin

CONTENTS

Chapter One

Life is NOT a Fairytale

Chapter Two

Meet the Mangleworts

Chapter Three

Vicious Vermina

Chapter Four

Glitz and Glam

Chapter Five

Midnight Magic

Chapter Six

The Munching Maid

Chapter Seven

If the Shoe Fits

LIST OF CHARACTERS

Buckle

Stomp

Cinderella

The Prince

Vermina

Nettle

With a special
appearance from
The Fairy Godmother

Chapter One
Life is NOT a Fairytale

"Yee-ouch!" I cried, as a burst of jabbing pain shot through me.

Buckle, my sister, glared at me with as much eyeball power as she could muster.

"It hurt!" I hissed. "You'd feel the same way if you stepped on a darning needle, sister dear." I stuck out my tongue and glared back at her with an equally sour scowl.

Now, before I carry on, I ought to tell you something...

My name is Stomp. I'm a shoe—a left shoe. And Buckle, my other half, is a right shoe. We aren't just any old shoes.

In fact, we belong to Cinderella.

You might already know the story. It's one of those rags to riches fairy tales. And in our case, it certainly was rags because we were a little down-at-the-heels—literally.

Anyway, let's get on with the story…

I could still feel the tingle in my sole, so I stepped carefully to the side. I was worried I'd tread on another needle.

You see, I'm unlucky like that. But I was so busy looking at the floor that I banged into the leg of the table.

Buckle glared at me again. "You're disturbing me," she sneered.

I was expecting Cinderella to bend down and rub me, but she didn't.

"That's a posh frock she's making," said Buckle, straining to look over the table above us.

"A what?" I said.

"A posh frock," said Buckle. "You know—a dress for best."

Buckle was right. The dress was a real stunner! Cinderella hummed as she stitched sequins carefully onto blue satin material. She sounded happy for once.

I'd seen the invitation to the Prince's ball a few days ago when Cinderella dropped it on the floor.

But I knew **Cinderella** wouldn't be happy for long. That was impossible while living with the step-family she'd had the misfortune to be given when her dad married again.

Cinderella's new stepmother, the foul Mrs. Manglewort, had two unpleasant daughters, Nettle and Vermina.

Someone slammed the heavy wooden front door. Like a wobbly echo, the vibrations shot through the hallway into the kitchen floor, making me feel queasy.

"Oh, Cinderella!" hollered one of her horrid Ugly Stepsisters. "Where are you?"

I cringed. Buckle raised her eyes at me. I raised mine back in agreement.

The one thing we were united on was Cinderella's extended family, who were just about bearable in small doses.

"Oh dear," said Cinderella.

Two enormous shadows loomed in the hallway. I looked up as a short, stout woman came barging in. Before she could heave herself completely through the door frame, a tall woman resembling a string bean pushed her to the side.

It was the Ugly Stepsisters.

"Vermina! Nettle!" said Cinderella as she quickly stuffed the ball gown into the cupboard behind her. Luckily, they were too distracted to notice Cinderella's lovely dress.

"Move back," shouted Nettle, the sister impersonating the string bean.

"This is getting ridiculous," said Vermina, trying to elbow her sister aside. "It's even become a competition to get through the door."

"Naughty, naughty Vermina," said Nettle with a grin. "You should let your elders and betters go first."

"I couldn't agree more," replied Vermina. "Age before beauty?"

"Nice try, dear sister," said Nettle. "I'm the whole package. Now, where is that little stepsister of ours?"

"I'm here!" said Cinderella as she quickly picked up the broom and began to sweep.

"Ah, our delightful stepsister," said the sisters, entering the kitchen. "We've got a surprise for you, Cinderella."

"A surprise for me?" Cinderella was completely shocked.

"Yes, just for you," said the sisters.

"We'd like the bathroom cleaned," said Nettle. "I had an accident with the talcum powder."

"But first we'd like our dinner cooked," said Vermina, giggling. "The lunch you made was tiny. I'd like a bigger plateful this time."

I hoped that Cinderella would stand up to them, but she didn't. Her spirit had been worn away, waiting for her dad to return. We'd been stuck with the Mangleworts ever since he'd gone off to look after his mother, leaving us in their care.

It was obvious—even to us, her shoes— that Cinderella missed her father very much.

Toilet (Talc) Powder

For those delicate ladies who sweat.

Directions: Apply liberally to all problem areas, such as feet, armpits, and buttocks

"Why do you pick on me?" Cinderella jumped as I squeezed hard on her toe.

"Don't bother asserting yourself," said Vermina with a sneer. "It isn't worth it. There are winners, dear Cinderella..."

"And losers," said Nettle with a toothy grin.

"Some people are lucky," said Vermina.

"And some people are not so lucky," said Nettle. "And you, my dear, are in the last category." Then they turned their backs to leave, fighting as they left the kitchen.

"Excuse me, dear sister, but it's *my* turn to go first," said Vermina, thrusting her ample shoulders forward.

"I think not," said Nettle, grabbing Vermina's hair and pulling her out of the way.

Finally, both of them squeezed through the door. They turned back towards Cinderella.

"Dinner first, then clean out the bathroom!" shouted Vermina, and both of them disappeared upstairs.

Cinderella got to work. While fixing supper for her awful step-family, she pulled out a large handkerchief, and was soon dabbing her eyes with it.

"Oh, no. Here we go again," I thought. Cinderella was crying.

But to my surprise, Buckle was also crying. Little water drops welled up in the corner of her eyes. With a shock, I realized it was the first burst of family warmth that I'd felt towards her in a long time. It was unlike her to feel sorry for someone else.

"Buckle, what's wrong?" I asked.

"Awful smell," said Buckle, wrinkling up her nose.

"Smell?" I asked, then sniffed the air. No wonder Buckle was crying.

Cinderella was peeling onions!

Chapter Two
Meet the Mangleworts

Cinderella slid the casserole dish into the oven. The pot scraped across the rungs, scratching the carefully polished metal.

While dinner was cooking, Cinderella took out a bottle of cleaner and a scrubbing brush from the cupboard. Then she went upstairs to clean the bathroom.

As she passed by Vermina's bedroom door, she could hear the gruesome two-some talking. They had two favorite hobbies. One was picking on Cinderella, their younger and prettier stepsister. The other was to pamper and preen themselves before going out to look for rich husbands. They were doing this now, checking themselves in the mirror and comparing their looks.

"Do you think I look pretty? Dare I say beautiful?" asked Vermina, twirling round.

"Oh, yes. You're beautiful even with those blotches on your face and that frightful expression," Nettle replied with a grin. "You look more like a ferret that crossed the road and didn't look where it was going."

"What about me, Vermina, do you think I look like an oil painting?" Nettle said, fluffing up her hair.

"Oh yes, oil," agreed Vermina. "Oil that's cooked a thousand fish 'n' chip suppers."

Nettle gave an unpleasant smile, and checked her face in the mirror. Perhaps her sister was right—she needed more fresh air. Her skin did have a slight greenish tinge to it.

Neither of the Ugly Stepsisters were a cheerful sight in the cold light of day. Nettle was stretched thin, with a sharp face and beakish nose, while Vermina was short and squat, with little piggy eyes.

"You're just jealous, sister dear," said Vermina. "You don't want me looking my best because I'm better looking than you."

"To the contrary, my sweet sibling," said Nettle, brandishing a pair of large silver tongs under her sister's nose. "You are welcome to borrow my nasal hair tweezers anytime!"

As Cinderella went downstairs to get another bottle of cleaner, she overheard her stepmother in the lounge. Mrs. Manglewort was boring her visitors by showing them the family photograph albums. She regularly performed this ritual when people came to visit.

"Here the girls are having fun," said Mrs. Manglewort, showing her guests a picture of Vermina spinning Nettle above her head.

"Fun?" said one visitor. "They're fighting! "

"I agree," said the second guest. "Your eldest daughter is about to be tossed like a javelin! Or is Vermina weightlifting?"

"Both my daughters also enjoy doing creative hobbies like needlework, gardening, and fencing," said Mrs. Manglewort, ignoring her visitors' comments.

Cinderella sighed.

The household chores never stopped. Even when she'd finished, more would miraculously appear. She was forever cooking, cleaning and washing. She was very pretty, but she didn't have time for her appearance because she was always at her stepsisters' beck and call.

"Cinderella, get me some breath mints," Nettle would say. "You made onion curry for supper on purpose."

"Cinderella, I want a snack," was always Vermina's demand. "Get it for me. Now!"

This is where I come in.

Cinderella wasn't the only one with a hard luck story. Because Cinderella was always working, her clothes were worn out. That included us, her trusty footwear.

Personally, I would have preferred to have been one of Dorothy's red slippers in the Wizard of OZ, or a handmade shoe in the Elves and the Shoemaker. Even if I'd been in the story of the Pied Piper of Hamelin then things would have been different.

But like the Ugly Stepsisters said, "In life, there are winners...and there are losers."

And that's how I felt— like a loser.

Ahh, how lovely...

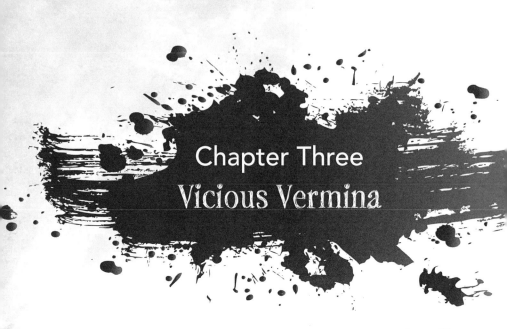

Chapter Three
Vicious Vermina

The thing is, I did feel sorry for Cinderella. But she wasn't the only one having a rough time with her family. I found Buckle, my sister, to be very disagreeable at times.

For some reason, though we'd had the same upbringing, I hadn't worn as well. Buckle seemed to sail through life unscathed, while life had left its mark on me.

I'm only a shoe, but I do have a sole—even if it was falling off. It seemed that when bad luck came around, I always got the biggest portion.

If someone stamped on Cinderella's toe, it was me that got crushed.

If Cinderella trod in something, it was me that stepped in it.

Squelch!

I'm so shiny!

I even got the uglier foot, too! And when the foot deodorant ran out, it was always on the foot that was in my shoe.

I knew that Buckle thought my misfortunes were funny.

"It's only because you're in the right place at the right time," I told my sister shoe. "If you were the left shoe for a change, then perhaps you'd understand."

Splat!

A dollop of some drudged up dinner Cinderella was preparing hurtled towards me. I jumped to the side and it landed on the floor beside me. A lucky miss!

But the second blob hit its target. Me!

As lovely as Cinderella was, cooking was not one of her best talents. The only thing that kept her interest these days was working on her dress for the Prince's upcoming ball.

I'd warned her a few times. But when she was busy stitching at material, she would completely forget all about the oven.

"Pay attention up there," I said, but Cinderella was focused, in the zone again. She didn't smell the smoke until it was too late.

"Ooh, what's that smell?" said Vermina, wrinkling up her squashed pink nose.

All three Mangleworts came bursting through the front door at the worst possible time.

Cinderella was caught working on her dress when she was supposed to be making her awful family a delectable dinner.

"Oh, Mummy," said nasty Nettle. "She's burnt our supper again! Can't we go to that new restaurant where they deep-fry everything, even dessert?"

Mrs. Manglewort looked furious. She agreed that they would all go out to eat, and that Cinderella could feast on the disgusting burnt dinner that went outside to cool.

"But first, she should make us a snack for the ride," said Vermina. "I'm wasting away."

The Mangleworts left in a hurry, which was just fine with me. For some reason, Vermina had an extra big smile on her round cheeks.

As soon as they were gone, Cinderella decided to go right back to working on her dress, but she couldn't find it anywhere.

"Where did my dress go?" asked Cinderella, looking puzzled. "I've nearly finished making it."

I remembered Vermina's smile.

"Check the oven," I said with a sigh.

At the time, I thought it was strange seeing a broom in her stepsister's pudgy hands. I thought that her awful step-sibling was trying to help for a change.

But, no. Vermina was simply doing what she did best.

Vicious Vermina had put
an end to Cinderella's
ballroom dreams.

Chapter Four
Glitz and Glam

Cinderella held up the torn and blackened ball gown. Her hopes of going to the party of the year had just been dashed.

I was a little surprised that Cinderella was so shocked that her stepsister had done this. It was nothing unusual for that mean pair.

Buckle and I staggered back so Cinderella could sit down and rub her eyes.

I understood how she felt. It was only natural that a girl should want to look her best at a royal ball. It was too late to find another outfit now.

After all this time, putting up with all the awful treatment from the Ugly Stepsisters, I'd never seen Cinderella this upset—puffy red eyes, a leaky snot-faucet, bawling away.

I hoped that her runny nose wouldn't drip down on me. It was a mean thought, I know, but I really wasn't in the mood for anything else falling on me.

WHOOSH!

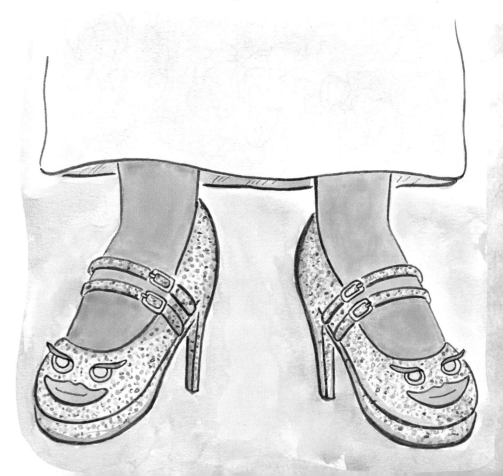

From out of nowhere, a pair of strappy, jeweled shoes appeared toe to toe with me. For a moment, I was blinded by the flash of sequins as they sparkled in the light of the kitchen fire.

Buckle pouted her lips. "Who are they?" she asked, equally surprised.

My sister had been upstaged by a pair of real dazzlers!

"Look up," said the high heels.

We looked up, past the glistening silver dress. Then past the shimmer of several golden necklaces, until we reached a smiling face with gleaming, magical eyes, topped with wavy silver and black hair.

This lovely lady had appeared just in time.

"Who are you?" said Cinderella to the vision in front of her. "Have you lost your way? Everybody has left for the Prince's ball. The whole town is going."

"I'm your **Fairy Godmother**," said the sparkly lady. And when she gave a shake of her hand, glittering flecks of purple and silver whirled around the heart-shaped wand.

"**Fairy Godmother**?" stammered **Cinderella**. "Why are you here?"

"For the past hour, you've been upset over some ball," said the **Fairy Godmother**. "I could hear you crying all the way from Fairyland."

"But why today of all days, **Fairy Godmother**?" asked **Cinderella**. "I've cried many times before this, and you've never shown up. My Ugly Stepsisters are always horrid. I wouldn't recognize them any other way."

"Because tonight is a special night," said the **Fairy Godmother**. "And one that will not come again. This is the one night that will change your life!"

"Yes, but you're too late. I've got nothing to wear," said **Cinderella**, holding up the ruined ball gown. "And how will I get there?

We live at the end of the village, and the buses stop running at eight. The Mangleworts have hidden all the money somewhere in the house, so I can't get a taxi."

The Fairy Godmother thought for a moment. Then she began to wave her wand around wildly, saying strange words.

"DINGLE DANGLE DINGLE DEE!

"WHIZZO WINGLE WHIZZO WHEE!

"FLIPPITY FLAPPITY FLIPPITY FLOP!

"TIPPITY TOPPITY RIPPITY ROP!"

I felt a strange sensation as my sides contracted and expanded. It felt like I'd been puffed up like a balloon.

"Buckle, help!" I cried. "I've got enough creases already. Another crack and I'll completely fall apart!"

By the look on her face, Buckle wasn't feeling too good, either.

Ribbit! Ribbit! Ribbit!

"Oh, no!" cried Buckle. "Cinderella's been turned into a toad!"

I was mortified. I didn't enjoy being a worn-out shoe, but I certainly didn't want to spend my days swimming around a pond.

"Sorry! Wrong spell," said the Fairy Godmother, then she chanted another one.

"GRIBBLE GROBBLE
"GRUBBLE GRIB!

"HIBBLE HOBBLE
"HUBBLE HIB!"

"WHIPPITY WHAPPITY
"WHOOPITY WOPP!

"SUPPITY SAPPITY
"SIPPITY SOPP!"

Everything went BLACK.

Then I was back in the room.

One minute I was a worn-out old running shoe, the next a shiny glass slipper. It was like having a makeover done at top speed. We went from *blah-blah-blah* to *ooh-la-la* in the blink of an eye!

The **Fairy Godmother** had granted **Cinderella's** wish. Her rags had been turned into a stunning ball gown. She would go to the dance after all!

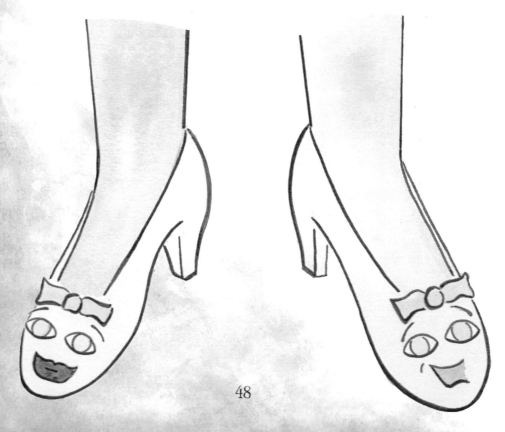

"Doesn't Cinderella look gorgeous," said Buckle, preening herself. "And I don't look bad myself."

A sarcastic remark was about to fall from my lips, but then I remembered that—for once—I also looked gorgeous. And it felt brilliant!

"Yes, Buckle," I said, sincerely. "You look stunning as a slipper. Every time you turn, your glass sparkles in the light."

My sister was too wrapped up admiring herself to notice that we now resembled the identical twins that we once were. Both shiny and new, without a mark on either of us.

I could see my reflection in Buckle's glass. I thought I must be dreaming. I swayed a bit. Being used to my lowly position in life, I didn't like heights.

"This is great," said Buckle. "But we'll have to get used to being fancy heels."

Buckle wobbled for a moment, but regained her composure. Soon she was gracefully gliding along. I tried to match her effortless movement, but I felt a little odd walking with my rear end stuck in the air.

Cinderella wrapped a stole around her shoulders. Then the Fairy Godmother took us outside.

A regal coach was parked in the driveway.

"Where did this come from?" I said, looking at the majestic vehicle with flames painted on the sides. Our tricked-out ride had gigantic tires made of the biggest pumpkins.

"Who's the coachman at the front?" I asked. "He looks like a frog!"

The Fairy Godmother said, "Cinderella, I took the largest vegetables in the garden and turned them into this rockin' carriage. Then I took a frog from the pond to make your driver."

I whispered to Buckle my concerns about a frog driver, but my sister shoe ignored me.

"But remember, Cinderella, that you must be back at the house by midnight tonight," said the Fairy Godmother. "That's when everything will return to normal."

As we climbed into the coach, the Fairy Godmother blew us a kiss. Then with another wave of her wand...she was gone.

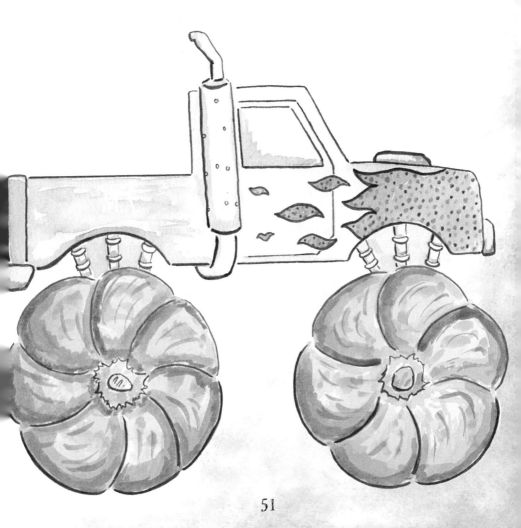

Cinderella, Buckle and I sat back to enjoy the ride. The coach gently bumped up and down over the cobblestones as it followed the winding streets to the palace.

Once we arrived, I couldn't wait to get to the ballroom.

As we carefully exited the carriage, using a stepladder, we looked up at the royal building. It looked magnificent! Hundreds of twinkling fairy lights glittered and shined under the pale moonlit sky. As we got closer, we could hear excited chatter coming from the gardens.

We walked along the path, which was lined with brightly colored lanterns. Music danced on the evening air.

I looked at Buckle and grinned.

She grinned back.

It

was

party

time!

Chapter Five
Midnight Magic

As we entered the ballroom, the first people we saw were the Ugly Stepsisters, who had positioned themselves at the refreshment table.

The Ugly Stepsisters were busy cramming food into doggy bags to take home. Vermina looked peeved because Nettle grabbed the last of the caviar, then smeared it onto a hot dog. She scanned the table for the next most expensive treat.

As her sister turned around and began slicing into a ham and pineapple pizza, Vermina flicked a large blob of mayonnaise at her back. It dribbled satisfyingly down her mustard yellow dress, creating a greasy stain.

"Steer *left*!" I hissed at Buckle. But it was okay because the sisters didn't recognize us. The **Fairy Godmother** had completely transformed Cinderella from kitchen drudge to Belle of the Ball.

The floor was quite slippery. The maids had spent the morning polishing it. The wooden boards felt silky to walk on. We kept slipping and sliding as we walked across the room.

The Prince had shelled out some big bucks for the best band in the country, Uggy Ugg and the Boulders.

The music was rockin'!

"I do beg your pardon," said Buckle as she came tip to tip with a red court shoe.

The room was crammed full of feet. Some of the more sturdy ones stood at the side, making polite conversation. The party-goers were twirling, swirling and whirling around the dance floor.

The stilettos strutted with style!

The pumps pranced with panache!

The sandals sashayed and grooved!

As for me, I was a little less nifty with my dance moves. I was out of practice.

"Sorry, Buckle," I said, wobbling about. I stifled a giggle. "It's taking me a while to find my feet!"

"Do you take anything seriously?" said Buckle. "I know how clumsy you are. You heard what the **Fairy Godmother** said: This ball could change our lives. Now, dance properly."

"Change our lives?" I replied. "But how? She also said the magic ran out at midnight, remember?"

Suddenly I was interrupted by a rather handsome boot.

"Please, excuse me," said the boot.

"Why? Did you burp?" I said, trying to be funny.

"He's asking you to dance," said Buckle in her usual grumpy tone.

I raised my eyes upwards at the well-dressed, posh dude talking to Cinderella.

"Who's that?" I asked.

"It's the Prince," said the boot. "It's his ball. And this is my other half."

Whussup, ladies?

Buckle gleamed with delight. She gave me a wink that said, "Now you're talking!"

From then on, it seemed as if we stayed with the Prince all night long.

We waltzed! We jigged! We tangoed! We discoed! We did the polka! And the foxtrot! We jived! We sambaed! We just danced and danced, then pranced and pranced.

We whirled the hours away.

"Buckle, are you getting tired yet?" I said, trying not to limp.

"No," she said.

Every shoe in the palace was getting smellier and more ripe by the minute. And so were that posh Prince's boots. But neither the handsome Prince or Cinderella seemed to mind. They only had eyes for each other.

Cinderella seemed to have lost track of the time altogether. Her mind had turned into crumbled Cheesie Toots crackers, smitten with the Prince.

I squeezed my sides in a few times to pinch Cinderella's toes, but she just rubbed her foot and carried on dancing.

The evening was flying by. Even Buckle was slowing down. There was less swagger in her stomp and less bounce in her boogie.

The clock struck twelve o'clock.

It was midnight.

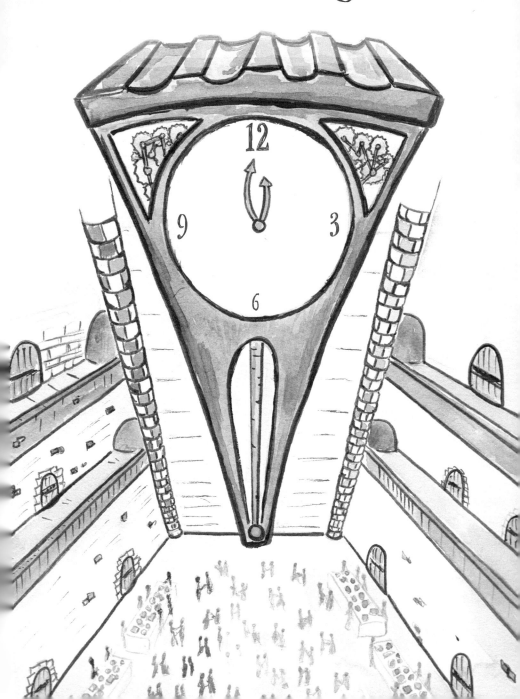

Cinderella froze in mid-strut. One arm was up in the air, the other down by her side. She looked like a child playing a tree in a school play.

"What's the matter?" asked the Prince.

A second chime struck, and Cinderella began to run.

Buckle and I faltered a little bit. As glass slippers, we certainly did look glamorous. But now, I realized that a running shoe was far more practical. If Buckle or I stumbled, Cinderella could twist her ankle, or trip up and fall flat on her face.

Ka-Dong! Sha-Bong!

Two more clock chimes sounded as we raced out of the ballroom and sprinted down the pathway to the coach. What had been loud music and happy chatter began to fade into the background, changing into a quiet hum the further away we got from the palace.

On the seventh chime of the clock, we reached our carriage.

Buckle and I jumped up into our seat, but the coach melted back into a pumpkin.

Ker-splickity-splat!

The ninth chime rang out.

Cinderella kicked up her heels to run down the path. But Buckle flew straight off her foot! She bounced once, and then landed in the road.

The tenth chime rang out.

Cinderella's beautiful dress was dissolving into the shabby old overalls she always wore. Dribbles of cooking fat were streaked across the sides where she'd wiped her hands, and a splash of custard on the strap was a sharp reminder of our real life back with the Mangleworts.

By the twelfth chime of the clock, we had completely changed back into the old Cinderella and the old Stomp.

"Stop! We've lost Buckle!" I shouted, but Cinderella was too busy concentrating on getting home.

Buckle was
left behind...
in the gutter.

Finally, we reached home. Cinderella opened the front door. The house looked the same as when we'd left it a few hours earlier. There was a glow of orange in the grate, as the fire began to fade. The oven, as usual, would need cleaning again in the morning.

I would really ache when I woke up. I had certainly been stretched and pushed into shapes I'd never been in before.

And so, just as the Fairy Godmother had said, the magic had disappeared at midnight.

For once, I was glad to be just an old comfortable running shoe again.

Before Cinderella went to sleep, she pushed me under the kitchen table. Then she went quietly up the stairs to her room.

As I lay there in the dark, all I could think about was Buckle.

My sister shoe... was gone!

Upstairs, I heard Cinderella crying herself to sleep. I did the same. Although my sister and I didn't always get along, I missed her terribly.

She was undoubtedly annoying, but I realized that as a single shoe, I would be tossed out. What use would I be to anyone?

A fly swatter, maybe? Spending my time squashing revolting creepy crawlies.

A door stop? A boring life that revolved around keeping something open.

To avoid that unfortunate end, I'd have to spend the rest of my lonely, single life, hiding at the back of the closet.

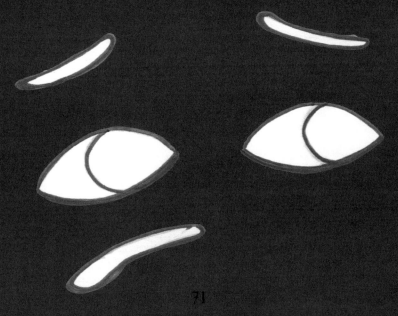

Chapter Six
The Munching Maid

BRRING! BRRING!

Nettle's alarm clock woke up the whole house. Cinderella had been up for hours, cleaning. Her face was marked by dark circles under her eyes, and she was wearing her slippers.

The Ugly Stepsisters came downstairs and demanded breakfast. Nettle nibbled her baked beans on toast, while Vermina crunched loudly on her all-in-one mega breakfast: a dozen fried eggs, Stargazy pie, and kipper flavored muffins.

I kept myself hidden under the table, but I wanted to see what was going on.

"Nettle, dear, who was that gentleman you danced with last night at the party?" said Vermina. "Very good looking, but with a terrible gas problem. All those foul noises..."

"You're one to talk, Vermina dear," said Nettle. "What about your dance partner? He was a knockout—certainly with his rotten breath, that is."

RICH MEN WELCOME!

The Mangleworts

There was a knock at the front door.

"Nettle! Vermina! Answer the front door," shouted Mrs. Manglewort. "I'm in the loo! I've got an upset stomach."

"Mummy, I told you not to eat the prune trifle last night," Vermina shouted back.

Nettle peered through the spy hole. Then she stepped back, looking very surprised.

"It's the Prince!" said Nettle. "What can he want?"

"Quick!" said Vermina. "Stall him! Don't let him leave! Just give me a moment. I need to check my face."

"We're just coming!" Nettle shouted through the keyhole.

The Ugly Stepsisters had a quick preen and primp in their hand mirrors. They were just about to open the door when they remembered...

Cinderella.

They shoved her into the pantry, and then rushed back to the front door. Putting the sweetest smiles on their horrible faces, they opened the door.

"Good morning," said the Prince, politely offering a groovy hang loose sign.

Vermina and Nettle invited him inside, and took him to the sitting room.

I was curious to see what he wanted. I crept along the hall and peeked around the doorway.

The **Prince** talked while the Ugly Stepsisters gazed at him, practically drooling all over themselves. He told them about the events of last night, and how he had met this wonderful girl.

"But she simply disappeared," explained the **Prince**. "I tried to follow her, but only found one of her glass shoes. I've tried a lot of girls already today, but none of their feet fit inside the slipper."

The **Prince** pulled out the shoe to show them.

It was Buckle!

I was so glad to see her. Although, after the events of last night, she was looking a little limp, and her glass had lost its shine. She was going to feel even worse when she realized what the **Prince** had in store for her.

I looked at **Vermina** and Nettle. Both were already removing their right shoes, and jostling to try Buckle on.

First, Nettle presented her foot. It was gnarled and bumpy like a road map.

"I'm afraid this shoe doesn't fit you," said the Prince.

In a state of high amusement, Vermina snorted her tea all over the table.

"My foot must have swelled up," said Nettle.

Buckle grimaced as the Prince tried to pull her off. She had never been this close to Nettle's feet before, and it wasn't a pleasant experience.

I think I'm going to be sick...

"Now it's my turn," said Vermina. She extended her plump pink foot forward. Her sharp toenails were supremely *funk-ay*.

Vermina puffed and panted as she tried to force her foot inside of Buckle.

"It doesn't fit you, either," said the Prince.

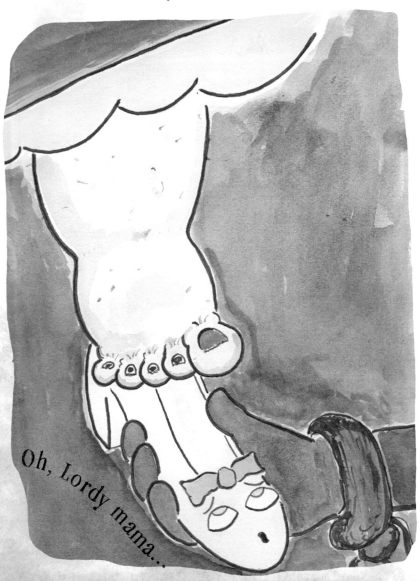

Oh, Lordy mama...

"I think you'll see that it *does*," said Vermina. Then she tried to squeeze it further into Buckle. Her face turned purple from squeezing so hard.

The Prince stopped for a moment. Perhaps the shoe did fit Vermina? He peered closely at her. She didn't look like the girl he had danced with last night. He knew she had been dressed up, but surely no amount of makeup could make *that* much difference.

I mustered all the eyeball power I could and willed Buckle to do something. For once in her life to be more than just a pretty face.

To my surprise, she did. She sucked in her sides so they pinched Vermina's foot even tighter.

"Get if off!" said Vermina, grimacing in pain as she tugged her foot out.

"I think you've had a lucky escape, Prince," said Nettle, trying not to laugh. "My sister's feet are smellier than the ripest cheese in the kitchen."

Vermina glared at her. "How dare you," she said, then tried to motion her older sister to be quiet. But Nettle had clearly forgotten that they'd hidden Cinderella in the kitchen.

The last thing they needed was the Prince discovering their *hot tamale* of a stepsister.

A noise came from within the kitchen pantry. It was a rustling sound. Actually, it was more of a crunching, munching sound.

MMMMMMMM....
These are SOOOO good...

Chapter Seven
If the Shoe Fits

"YUMMM," said a muffled voice.

"Who's that?" asked the Prince. "Is someone else in the house with you?"

"Only the maid," said Vermina.

"The servant girl, Cinderella," said Nettle.

The Ugly Stepsisters both groaned when they realized their mistake.

"Let me have a look," said the Prince.

He pushed past Vermina and Nettle and opened the pantry door.

Cinderella's startled face peered out. She had cracker crumbs all around her mouth. Not to mention the old, shabby overalls she was wearing, and smears of grease in her hair.

"Are you the maid?" asked the Prince.

Cinderella was a little embarrassed. She started fanning herself with the empty box of delicious Cheesie Toots crackers.

"Wait a minute," said the Prince. "I recognize your loveliness from last night. It's you! You're the girl I danced with at the ball."

The Ugly Stepsisters looked furious.

"I thought you said you'd gotten rid of Cinderella's ball gown," said Nettle to Vermina. "Can't you do anything right?"

"The Glass Slipper," I said, and then gave a loud cough.

"What?" said the Prince.

"The Glass Slipper," I said, louder this time.

"Ah, yes, I almost forgot—the Glass Slipper," said the Prince. "Try this on, and let's make it official."

Cinderella stretched out her foot. I couldn't bear to look. But of course, Buckle slid easily onto Cinderella's foot.

It was a perfect fit.

"Whoop-Whoop!" cried the Prince. He did a little dance, wiggling his royal behind around. Then he planted a large, wet kiss on Cinderella's cheek and punched the air with his fist.

"My search was worth it," said the Prince. "When you left the ball, I tried to follow you, but all I found was your shoe. Now, at long last, I've found my Mrs. Charming-to-be!"

"Let's go
out and...
celebrate!"

ow...leg cramp...

The Prince was so happy that he tossed poor Buckle up into the air.

My sister shoe flew up to the ceiling, somersaulting as she went. On the descent, she was rather more ungainly, and plummeted downwards like a sack of stones. I looked around for the Prince, but he was on his way out the door.

"Isn't there something you've forgotten?" I shouted to him quickly, trying to indicate the airborne Buckle. There was no time to lose. Any second now, she'd hit the floor.

The Prince ignored me. He was too wrapped up in his thoughts about his future with Cinderella.

The happy couple rode away without a care in the world. So much for a handsome Prince and sugar sweet Cinderella.

My sister was in bits!

"I'm not cleaning that mess up," said Nettle. "It's your fault, Vermina. You do it."

"Why should I clean it up?" said Vermina, and they both stamped out of the room to get their mother to take sides.

Thank goodness the Ugly Stepsisters hadn't wanted to clean up. Otherwise, Buckle would have been swept up and thrown in the rubbish. And I would have been thrown in after her.

After everyone had left, I came out and looked sadly at the pieces of glass glinting on the floor. Then I shut my eyes and wished.

I wished for anything, really. That the Prince had a handsome older brother and he was coming to save us. That none of this sad story had happened in the first place, or that I would discover that the Fairy Godmother had left her wand behind the bread bin, and that I too could have some magic in my life.

I opened my eyes.

No such luck.

I was still a worn-out old shoe, and my sister was a pile of broken glass.

Whoosh!

There was a flash of glitzy gold and ruby red. Then I found myself staring at a pair of gold flip-flops.

"Where did you come from?" I asked.

"From the story of Aladdin," the sandals replied. They both nodded upwards at the sparkly gentleman. "You know, the story about the genie who lives in a magic lamp."

"But this story is about Cinderella!" I said.

"If I were you, I wouldn't worry about that," said one gold flip-flop, the left one. "I'm here to grant you a wish."

"Just one?" I said. "I thought genies grant three wishes."

"Hey, you're an unlucky shoe, remember?" said the other gold flip-flop, the right one. "You only get one wish."

One wish was better than none. It was our last chance for Buckle and I to be reunited again. But not just that, I had a thought...

I cleared my throat and said, "My wish is for Buckle and I to be the ruby slippers in the Wizard of Oz."

"As you wish," said the genie.

"But just so you know..." The genie gave me a look of warning. "During the opening scene, you'll make your entrance worn by the Wicked Witch of the East. She'll be knocked flat by Dorothy's house, which has spun out of control. And there's an awful lot of walking to do along the Yellow Brick Road."

I thought about the situation. The rubbish bin or the Wizard of Oz. There wasn't a lot of choice, really.

"You're on!" I said, and gave a heels-up. It would've been a thumbs up, but as I'm a shoe, I don't have a thumb, or even toes.

There was a puff of smoke.

Then a loud BANG!

Then...

Once again, I felt strange as my sides expanded and contracted.

Voila!

Buckle and I were transformed into a pair of ruby red slippers.

"Did I hear something about walking a long way?" said Buckle, a bit confused. "The last thing I remember is doing an acrobatic routine when the Prince went off with Cinderella."

"Don't worry about that for now," I said. "I'll explain as we go."

"I can't wait," said Buckle. "After all, it's not so bad being a shoe..."

"Well, you know what they say," I answered. "There's no business like shoe business! Now let's get outta here!"

But that's another Footwear Fairytale!

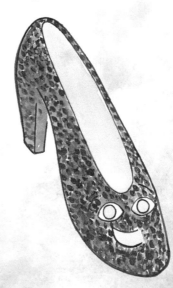

Until next time!

No matter where I go...
I'm so SHINY!

Philippa Rae

...has worked for and with children most of her life - as a dance teacher, youth worker, BBC radio producer, and now children's writer. She has also been involved in independent film-making, such as the Moondance International Film Festival, and charity projects.

Her picture book *Count the Sheep to Sleep* won a silver award at the Moonbeam Children's Book Awards.

Tevin Hansen

...is the author and illustrator of numerous books for young readers, and an editor for Stinkwaves magazine. He resides in Lincoln, Nebraska, with his wife and two kids,

Thank you for purchasing and reading
Cinderella's Other Shoe.

Handersen Publishing is an independent press dedicated to making quality, fast-paced books that kids (and parents) will enjoy reading. If you liked this book, we have many other titles available on Amazon or directly through our website:

www.handersenpublishing.com

We also hope that you will consider leaving a review on Amazon or Goodreads. A review can make a big difference to the little guy.

And please take a moment to check out our magazine, Stinkwaves, which is published twice a year.

www.stinkwavesmagazine.com

Thank you.

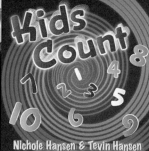
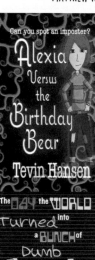
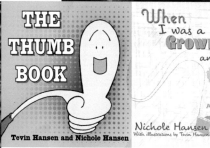